Tombstone Blues

also by Chadwick Ginther

Thunder Road

Tombstone Blues

By Chadwick Ginther

RaveN
STONE

Tombstone Blues
copyright © Chadwick Ginther 2013

Published by Ravenstone
an imprint of Turnstone Press
Artspace Building
206-100 Arthur Street
Winnipeg, MB
R3B 1H3 Canada
www.TurnstonePress.com

Turnstone Press gratefully acknowledges the assistance of the
Canada Council for the Arts, the Manitoba Arts Council, the
Government of Canada through the Canada Book Fund, and
the Province of Manitoba through the Book Publishing Tax
Credit and the Book Publisher Marketing Assistance Program.

Printed and bound in Canada by Friesens for Turnstone Press.

Library and Archives Canada Cataloguing in Publication

Ginther, Chadwick, 1975–, author
        Tombstone blues / Chadwick Ginther.

(Thunder Road trilogy)
ISBN 978-0-88801-445-0 (pbk.)

        I. Title. II. Series: Ginther, Chadwick, 1975– . Thunder
road trilogy.

PS8613.I54T64 2013   C813'.6   C2013-905183-X

For my parents, Charles and Sunday,
who in addition to all they've done for me,
gave me a love of books and reading.

Tombstone Blues

Prologue
Down Here
with the Rest of Us

"Give it time, dear one," his mistress said. "He is too igno-rant to know what else waits in the mist. He will call them again. And when he does... you will be free. You will have that which you desire—all that you desire. We shall have our revenge. Things will be as they were meant to be. The dead shall remain dead. Finally."

She reached up with a pale, delicate hand to stroke his ashen face. Her fingers cracked the crust of rime that buried his beard. Once, when he used to shrink from her touch, his beard had been as brilliant as a sunrise. Now, it was a dull, lifeless grey.

Dead.

Like him.

In time he had learned to love his place at her side. To crave even the briefest moment of intimacy and pleasure, things that were forever denied those who were dead. He knew, even offered his freedom, he would return to this place. To her.

Slowly, he clenched his gauntleted hand into a fist. The rusted metal of the iron glove creaked. He knew better than to touch her without her bidding. Many times since he had first been dragged into her realm, had the folly of *that* been made clear.

He used to worry about what his father would think, seeing him so, craving the touch of a once mortal enemy. It did not matter. Wherever his father had fallen, it was not this place, but somewhere not even wily Odin could escape. There was nowhere left for the gods now, nowhere but the mists of Niflheim, and within them, Hel, the Land of the Dead.

"Would you like to walk the world again?"

She was not addressing him this time, he knew, and that rankled. Instead she spoke to packed masses of the elderly and the sickly; the starved and cowardly dead. They sat at the tables of her hall with empty plates and goblets laid out before them.

"Would you feed upon their fear?" She could speak sweetly when she chose—when it suited her. "I believe you will. But you won't be alone. And you needn't walk."

Her grin touched only half of her face, where her lips were full, if cruel, and her skin alabaster. The other side, fire-blackened and scab-cracked, showed broken teeth and held no mirth. She held a hand out to him—her right. It was skeletal and black, like the ruin of her face. One might wonder: what could scar a goddess so? But she had been birthed with this countenance— half beauty, half nightmare. Even then, she'd straddled the worlds of life and death. Her true scar, he noted, had been left by her father. *And how that trickster had scarred them all.* Ignoring her injunction not to do so, he took her hand in his iron glove, crushing it in his grip.

She smiled at his impertinence. This time, her smile seemed

to reach her entire face. A sight he alone was allowed to appreciate. Guiding him, she placed his hand over the hollow where a breast had never been. Curdled milk wept over rust. He felt no heartbeat. Even before Odin had banished her beneath Midgard, there had been no breath of life in her. She was Hel, the goddess of the dead, and both her hall and the realm it dwelt within shared her dread name.

Rising from her throne, Hel beckoned, and he fell in at her side. The dead shrank back from them, clearing a path down the center of her hall. Some reached out; their fingertips raw where their nails had once been. Those wretches, he brushed aside.

They were nothing. Cowards all.

Woven serpents were the brick and mortar of her palace. Undulating in excitement, the walls dripped venom, snapping at any but their mistress. Any who dared tread too close. In his lady's bursting home, they need not reach far.

Shuffling in step behind their mistress, the dead followed in a shambling, hungry gait. Only on Midgard could they be sated. Fear became their meat and mead, terror their bread and beer. Temporary appeasement would make the starvation they faced upon their return all the more bitter. A feast turned to ashes. Some managed to gorge themselves so deeply that they were able to remain above as shades, lingering on as reminders of her power. They had slipped through his father's fence in ones, or even threes, but not in the numbers his mistress required.

Those above no longer believed. Not in *this* underworld. And too few knew his lady's name to make the proper observances. But they would learn.

There was one that knew.

That mortal knew all too much—Odin's ravens served Ófriður now, as did the Norns. They told him much, and yet he had foolishly taken what did not belong to him. Even worse, he had stolen from her.

Sliding the bolt—a *jötunn*'s severed finger—from the lock, she pushed open the gates to her realm. Icy, grey fog roiled just beyond the boundary between Hel and Niflheim. Floating on the cold fog, as if it was a gentle sea, a great longship was moored to the fence. A rotten wooden dock ran up to the ship. *Naglfar*. Pale, tattered sails draped limply from its mast, carved with curse upon curse. It didn't creak and groan as a wooden ship should; instead it squealed like bending iron and shuddered like a corpse expelling air.

Naglfar had been crafted from the fingernails of the dead. The ship had only been sailed once before. When the trickster—the betrayer—Loki, had steered it to Asgard to face his former brethren at Ragnarök. How he hated Loki. Not even the end of the world could sate his loathing for that turncoat little *jötunn*.

He stood there, seething. Once his anger would have set the clouds alight with fire, shaken the very foundations of Midgard. No longer. He could feel a storm brewing above in the world of mortals. This storm was not his doing. A low, animal growl rumbled in his throat. The storm was *his*. Perhaps the usurper already battled Hel's chosen. His mistress had sent her four mead maidens above, nightmares walked Midgard too. If the bitches robbed him of his prize, their torment would last an eternity. He would feed them to the mists of Niflheim in pieces. His hatred was the only warmth left to him in this cold, cold place.

"Go," she said to the dead. "Board *Naglfar*." And they did.

They poured from Hel, the realm of the dead that took its name from its queen. He watched as they passed the broken, one-handed man who had once called him brother. A wretched thing—barely recognizable as man, let alone a god. When his brother looked up at him with empty sockets, strangely still full of hate, he was glad his mistress had made him take out those eyes.

You would despise what I have become, Tyr, could you see me. Blindness was the only gift I could give you. Some colour still lit the eyeless god's face, and despite his emaciated form he spat with impotent defiance. Once—an eternity ago—they had been bound together at the gates of Hel. Side by side, brother to brother.

Whooping cries that held no joy arose as the dead stumbled aboard *Naglfar*. But still they went, climbing aboard the ship, and waiting for the call. *And when the thief calls to his "honoured" dead, we will be the ones to answer....*

A shrill cry echoed past the army of the dead. In the deepest depths of Niflheim dwelt the hungry dragon Níðhöggur, and greater, darker spirits, that even Hel would not welcome into her hall. Those spirits meant nothing. They could do nothing to stop them once the way was opened.

When his mistress patted his brother fondly he felt a stab of jealousy. Tyr stared empty death at his captor. The fool didn't even know when he was being honoured.

Hel jerked his brother's head back to expose his neck. Her tongue, red and black as if it were stained by fresh and rotted blood both, lapped at Tyr's neck before taking a bite. Ripping a small gobbet of flesh free, she spat it into the mist before turning away.

Back to her servant.

Now her touch was his, she drew him close and whispered, her breath rank with Tyr's blood. "When the horn sounds, unfurl the sails. Midgard will once again belong to you."

He nodded curtly and wished he could summon a chill wind to lift him aboard the ship. Instead his boots boomed over the dock as he boarded *Naglfar*. Pinpricks of light moved in the mist. He clenched his teeth as the fog swallowed them. Soon he would have his turn. Soon he would have his hammer back.

Soon Thor would ride the wild winds again.

1. Calling All Destroyers

This the one?" Ted yelled.

"Yeah, that's my work," Robin hollered back. "Kick his ass."

An elf waited between two poles in the dirty sand of a beach volleyball court in one of Winnipeg's civic parks. He traced a line with his foot, as if daring them forward. Ted didn't need an engraved invitation. He rushed the cocky little fucker.

Whirling away from Ted, the elf spun his spear in a broad arc. Ted wouldn't exactly call the elf human. A shade over five-foot with slender, sinewy arms and legs, the elf was mostly naked. Tattooed runes formed three linked triangles, pointing downward, bright against his too-white skin. His ears tapered to slight points and his hair flapped unbound like a matador's cloak.

He moved with inhuman speed. That shouldn't have surprised Ted, but it did. The spear darted. Ted hopped back on instinct. *An instinct I'll have to overcome if I want to get my hands on the little shit.* But even though he had a good foot over the elf, *height means fuck-all against the reach of that spear.*

He'd been hunting this damned thing for Robin for two damned months with no luck. His ravens had recognized the stink of an *álfur*, and in the circular fucking logic of magic, you could only find an elf's barrow if you already knew how to get there. Tracking the bastard to one of the parks had taken no time at all. Once inside, however, those two months of searching had left Ted and Robin with nothing to show for their efforts. Unfortunately for the elf, he'd found *them*.

Silver eyes flashed in the moonlight. Wood creaked and groaned. The elf's spear stretched, doubling its length, and clouted Ted behind the ear. His head should be ringing. He should be dropping to his knees, waiting for his vision to clear. But he was doing neither of those things. He was standing. Smiling.

Ted trapped the spear with his left hand and pulled, jerking both weapon and elf closer. The elf grunted in surprise as Ted swung a haymaker with his right hand. A stylized hammerhead tattoo decorated both the top and bottom of his forearm, ending at his knuckles. That tattoo was Mjölnir—the hammer of Thor, Norse god of thunder. And it hit just as hard.

At least it did when it connected.

As if alive, the spear coiled, snake-like, around Ted's legs, tripping him. He tumbled forward, gripping the spear, trying to use the elf to balance himself and keep his feet. The elf released the spear with a smile and Ted hit the sand.

"Now you've pissed me off, you hopping bastard."

Ted stood and bent the spear over his knee. Trying to break the weapon was harder than he'd expected. The spear had the spring of green, living wood. But it could only bend so far. Finally, the spear snapped with a crack. Sap sprayed from the frayed tendrils of wood. The sweet scent of the sap was undercut by a coppery tang. *Blood.* Maybe the spear was *alive*.

Ted cast it aside, trying not to shudder. "Bet you're not so bad without your little toy."

The elf smiled a queer little smile and drew a bone from a belt at his waist. Reaching up, he touched the bone to a shaft of moonlight that cut through the tree canopy. When he drew the bone free, the light followed, forming a curved sword blade; its steel glowing like an extension of the moon.

Ted shook his head. *Fucking magic.*

Robin yelled, "Look out!"

"Get back!" Ted said.

The elf grinned. In a blur, as if it had skipped from moonbeam to moonbeam without crossing the distance between, it was next to Robin. Lashing out with the glowing sword, the elf took Robin in the shoulder. As the sword came free from his body, no blood stained the blade, but he still fell.

Ted lunged forward, leading with his left forearm like it was a shield. The sword struck where tattooed metallic green scales covered him like a shirt. Scales that made Ted damn near invulnerable. Even a giant swinging full out hadn't been able to kill him. No fucking elf was going to hit near that hard. Ted forced the blade up and closed inside the elf's reach. Shifting his weight, the elf launched himself over Ted, spinning around an outstretched arm and landed behind him.

Fast little fucker.

Pivoting, Ted scythed his right arm backwards. There was a satisfying crack as the strike connected with the elf's ribs. The glowing sword pinwheeled free and the elf hit the sand with a groan. When he struggled to rise, Ted hit him again.

The impact drove the elf deeper into the ground, sending up a spray of sand.

Ted waited a moment. The elf didn't move. Ted jabbed a finger at him. "Stay down, Jumpin' Jack Flash, or you're never getting up."

He walked over to Robin and knelt at his side.

"You okay?" Ted asked.

"C-c-cold…" Robin forced past chattering teeth. "F-f-fucking cold."

It was warm for November in Winnipeg, but Robin's breath misted in front of him and he shuddered, crossing his arms over his chest. The sun tattooed on Ted's left palm began to glow with golden light; a pinprick of daylight in the dark of evening. Within that aura, Ted could see that Robin's lips and extremities had turned blue and his face ashen.

Ted pressed his palm over the wound. The light intensified, Robin gasped and shot straight up. Ted caught him before he slumped back down as the light faded. He knew from previous experience that a day would pass before he could use the healing warmth of the sun tattoo again.

The dwarves had not made him to play doctor.

They'd turned Ted from an unemployed divorcee into a weapon. *Their* weapon. They'd called the powers gifts—but Ted wasn't about to exchange Christmas cards with them any time soon. *Ófriður*, they'd named him. An Icelandic word. A word for war. Names, he was learning, were important in his new world.

"Thanks," Robin mumbled breathlessly, rubbing where the wound had been.

"Don't mention it."

"Shit!" the artist said, pulling at the side of the stained wife-beater he wore under his jacket.

"What's wrong?" Ted asked.

"My dragon tat. There's a blank spot where the damn sword cut me."

"So?" Though Ted's body was covered with at least as much ink as the artist's, he had no sentimental attachment to the images on his body. His powers were pretty cool, but they'd been carved—brutally—into him against his will.

"I had that dragon done in Japan, tapped out by hand." Robin's voice took on a lecturing tone, like he was about to explain something Very Important to a child. "The master who did it is dead, and nobody's going to work over *his* ink."

"You're alive. That's gotta count for something." Ted picked up the sword. It was still glowing softly. Huginn alighted on the elf's shoulder, Muninn on Robin's; the ravens cawed shrilly. "Now, let's find out what this fucker was up to when he came to your shop."

Robin was a tattoo artist. And a good one, from what Ted knew, but he wasn't the one who had covered Ted's body in ink. That dubious honour went to a group of dwarves—*dvergar* if you were into being technical. Dwarves that made Grumpy look like the Friendly fucking Giant.

Robin held a cigarette to his lips with a shaking hand. His eyes darted from one raven to the other. Sick yellow tar stains painted the artist's middle and index fingers. Ted doubted those fingers *hadn't* held a cigarette in the days since he'd called Ted.

13

This is indeed the álfur responsible, Huginn said. When the bird wasn't flying around, Huginn was also one of Ted's tattoos—a stylized raven image representing Thought.

Obviously, Muninn, Ted's other raven tattoo added. Muninn was Memory. Besides possessing the decidedly non-magical power to drive Ted crazy, the ravens were a wealth of knowledge about the Nine Worlds of Norse myth.

Chance and proximity had led Ted to the tattoo artist two months ago. He'd been the one Ted first asked to explain the meanings of his tattoos. Robin had given him some answers—and raised more questions. He'd promised Ted he'd do more research, but that wasn't why he'd called. Something had happened. Something bad. Robin's only memory after his last sitting of the night was seeing the sunlight creep across the street in front of the shop.

Ted felt bad about those days Robin had spent in fear and ignorance; nihilistic fire giants had a way of holding one's attention.

I will find what was taken from him, Huginn offered.

Not to be outdone, Muninn chimed in with: **And *I* can return what was taken *to* him.**

Together the ravens had been informers for Odin, the chief of the Norse gods. They would spend the day flying through the Nine Worlds and their nights upon the All-Father's shoulders, whispering their findings in his ears. Ever since the dwarves got hold of Ted, the ravens had whispered to him. He'd thought he was going crazy when they first started to speak. But shortly after, he was ass-deep in trickster gods, giants, and sea serpents.

Maybe I am a little crazy, but everything else in the Nine is bug-fuck nuts.

"This is going to be weird," Ted warned Robin.

"Right," the artist said. "'Cause losing a whole night is normal."

Back when Ted was working on the patch in Alberta, he'd lost more than his share of nights. He shrugged but didn't share.

"**Returning your lost memories will hurt,**" Muninn told Robin.

The artist's eyes went wider. He was shaking a little.

"It will?" he asked.

"**Yes,**" Muninn said.

"It's so weird that they talk," Robin said, clutching at the least-strange oddity before him.

Ted snorted. "Try and get them to shut the fuck up."

"Were they doing this—" Robin waved a hand at the two birds "—when you came to see me that first time?"

"Not yet," Ted said. "I thought I'd been hearing crows all day."

"**It took us some time to make it through that thick skull of his,**" Huginn said, flapping his wings to land on Robin's shoulder. The raven hopped side to side twice to settle itself. Muninn shortly followed.

"**It still can,**" Muninn said.

"Are they always like this?" Robin asked.

Ted nodded. "But sometimes they're *really* annoying."

"All right." Robin squinted his eyes shut, dread evident as his shoulders hunched tight. "Do what you have to do."

"**Relax**," Ted heard Huginn say. The word was overlapped with a soft croaking raven call.

"**Your last sitting has just walked in the door,**" Muninn said.

Robin shuddered, groaning. Ted heard the chime of the door opening as the ravens dredged up thoughts that weren't so much missing, as buried. The birds were the source of much of Ted's knowledge of the Nine Worlds. They'd shown him images of Ragnarök, of the adventures and follies of the gods and as they were returning Robin's stolen memories, they were also projecting those thoughts to Ted.

It had been an ordinary night at the shop, and Don, the shop manager, had wanted to cut out early.

Robin nodded and waved him off. "Lock the door when you leave," the artist said. "I don't want any drunk walk-ins."

He didn't mind working alone. He was down to his last appointment: an intricate Celtic Knot for a sweet little hardbody and he was taking his time to get the shading *just* right. She was tall and leggy; this was her first tat and the idea of *that* much canvas to work on was pretty appealing. The view didn't hurt either. He was still trying to convince his girlfriend to get her first tattoo.

The client had changed her mind since their first consult. He resolved to not think of her name. Something for his lips to say, but not for his mind to remember. Originally, the piece was to be nestled between her breasts, its top edge just visible over the neckline of her wedding dress. But the groom had a big mouth and his mom had made a huge stink about the whole thing.

"My mother-in-law can go fuck herself," the client said. "I'll get my tattoo somewhere the bitch will never see it." Somewhere just for her fiancé. Then she was going to make him beg just to get a peek.

Robin tried to talk her out of changing her mind. Though he didn't fight *too* hard.

It was awkward, spending the time hunched between the client's legs, and he wasn't sure what to tell Aiko when she asked how his day had been. His client had been pretty easygoing, and hadn't flinched at all when he'd got out the razor to do the necessary groundskeeping. She made some comments that to another man might have seemed an invitation to do more to her than just tattoo, or hint at the possibility she might be willing to have a bit of premarital fun. Nothing Robin hadn't heard before and he wasn't about to be baited. Tattooing can be quite intimate, and he was used to clients taking that to mean more than services rendered.

It was true he'd screwed around with more than his share of his clients in the past, *more pussy is better pussy,* he'd thought then. Robin also knew you never went for head in the shop until *after* they'd paid for the work. That way if they were putting you on, at least you had their money in your ass pocket when the indignant act started. He'd been burned once before. Never again. But there had been no one since he'd met Aiko, a fidelity that surprised him.

The door chimed open. He wouldn't have heard the noise if he hadn't turned down the music when Don had popped in to let him know he was leaving.

Probably forgot his damn iPod again.

Robin was just about to fill in the last of the shading when the woman jumped back. The paper covering the bench made a crinkling sound as her bare ass shifted.

She pawed for something to cover herself. Over the hours he'd been working she'd let him remove the towel that had been hiding the fork of her legs. It hadn't mattered to Robin. The towel wasn't awkward to work around. His hard-on, on the other hand… She pulled her knees up to her chest and wrapped her hands about her locked ankles. Her eyes were wide and she was shaking.

Robin whirled around.

It wasn't Don.

He blocked the stranger's view of his client. A heavy parka hung to the man's knees. It was way too early—and warm—for such a coat. His hands were stuffed in his pockets. His boots were Sorels, but had no laces. The man stank. Not the sour, unwashed smell of a street person, but sickly sweet, like honey left to ferment.

If Don forgot to lock the fucking door, he's gonna owe me for the tip I'll be losing on this. A client's desire to pay extra generally evaporated if a bum got a free show.

"Hey," he said, stepping forward. "This isn't a goddamn shelter. Get out." He moved to shove the bum, but the guy moved faster than Robin's eye could follow. Hands still stuffed in the pockets of the parka, he appeared to Robin's left. Robin blinked and the bum was already back where he'd originally stood.

No one should be able to move like that.

Robin started to sweat. The bum looked like a man, but hadn't moved like one. The whatever-it-was stepped out of the clothes as if it were moulting. It didn't undress; rather, it stepped forward, leaving its clothes to fall in a pile.

"What... what the hell are you?" Robin stammered.

As they caught the light, the intruder's eyes glittered like a wolf's. It was maybe five feet tall. Its skin was pale, so pale it glowed like moonlight, while its hair, which hung poker-straight, shone metallically, shifting as he moved like a thousand slender razors.

Robin shook. "Wha—what do you want?"

"Your expertise," it said, before looking at Robin's client. It licked its lips as if anticipating a meal. "The female can leave."

The client didn't need to be told twice. Her clothes were neatly piled on a nearby chair. She grabbed her jeans and ran bare-assed out the door. Even Robin couldn't fault her for running. Hell, *he* wanted to—run and run and never stop.

"I usually work by appointment," Robin said, swallowing hard. "And I'm booked solid right now."

He immediately wished he could take the words back. That he could learn for once to keep his big gob shut. Other than a sniff, the thing ignored the attempt at a joke. *Lucky*, Robin thought, exhaling deeply. Deliberately, the thing set down three stones on the cigarette package on Robin's workbench. Carved on each was one of the Norse elder runes. *That guy from Alberta—what was his name? Cullen? No, Callan. Tom? Ted.* Robin remembered the man's belief that he'd had ten years of work done in a night. All of that work Norse. He had the dude's number somewhere. He'd offered to research those tattoos and call the guy back. *If I don't get shivved, I'll definitely be giving Ted Callan a call.*

"I want this," the stranger said, unrolling a large translucent page that Robin realized with a shudder wasn't paper. He set the page on his workbench and placed two stones at the top and one on the bottom to keep it flat. The symbol drawn on the page was three interlocking triangles facing point down, one centred, the second offset down and slightly left, the third lower still and to the right. Looking closer, he saw that while each of the triangles appeared solid, in fact they were made of tightly packed runes— the three on the stones—repeated over and over.

Staring at the symbol made Robin's eyes lose focus, and he felt like he was being pulled into the image. He blinked, looked away, and said, "Uh, okay, that's cool man, cool. How do you plan on paying for this work?"

When the stranger smiled, his teeth were all filed to points. The grin reminded Robin of a serrated knife.

"Very wise of you to ask. Your life, as payment, perhaps? It is all I hold in my hand that is of value to the likes of you."

Over the years, Robin had seen all manner of weird shit in his nights at the shop and had a pretty good poker face. But he still wanted to piss himself when he looked at the stranger. The front door slammed. At least the client had gotten away.

Robin swallowed. "Where do you want your tat?"

"Here," it said, tapping its chest; in the fluorescent light of the room, its pale skin glowed, and Robin had a hard time making out any features or muscles on the stranger. "You will be done by sunrise or our deal is forfeit, and your life with it."

"I can't do that. No. What you're asking… is impossible."

The stranger glided forward. It jabbed two fingers under Robin's chin. He could feel his skin start to part beneath the thing's nails. Blood spattered the floor. "Pity."

I'm gonna die. "It's cool, it's cool. I'll make this work."

It patted his cheek with two terse slaps. "See that you do."

Robin set the tattoo machine down on his workstation. He realized he'd been holding the machine in front of him, like it was a shield. Instead, he pawed for a sharpie marker. There was no way he'd finish this tattoo before dawn if he tried to do transfers and stencils for the creepy fucker. He'd have to freehand the design.

Robin drew his first line starting at the stranger's right shoulder, across the clavicle and to the left shoulder. It was shaky going at first, but Robin found a measure of calm in the routine action. He finished the triangle, angling the lines to terminate at the belly button. The second triangle started below the pectoral and ran into the stranger's side before slashing down across ribs and to the groin. For the third, Robin bisected the right pectoral and into the underarm, down again over the ribs, the final point ending midway between the first two.

Beats dying.

"Got a colour in mind?" Robin asked.

"Red." He set down an intricate glass vessel on Robin's work bench. Thick, dark liquid swirled about, clinging to the glass. The stranger removed the stopper. "Use this."

Robin hissed through his teeth. When you're tattooing some-one, you're essentially jabbing them over and over again with needles. People tend to bleed when you poke them hard enough, so Robin had seen enough blood to know that the client's jar was full of it. He could smell the coppery tang over the stink of his own sweat, and the sick honey scent coming from the stranger.

Would it even work in his machine? The blood?

Robin was glad he was wearing gloves.

Fortunately, Norse runes aren't nearly as intricate as Kanji. Always straight lines, they'd been meant for carving in wood or rock, so they were designed to be perpendicular or diagonal lines that could never be mistaken for wood grain. If he'd been doing something more elaborate, he'd never finish what the guy was asking for by sunrise. Robin drew the three runes on the client's torso. If he was doing the image freehand he wanted them in sight at all times. He imagined *this* client would know the instant he screwed up.

Robin didn't bother with shading or thickening the lines. Each rune got one pass before he butted the next one up against it. The stranger sang and the rune stones glowed as oddly thin blue blood wept from the tattoos. The work gave the pale skin an angry purplish cast, like a fresh bruise. Robin's back began to ache and his bowels clenched. If he didn't have time for artistic integrity, there was no time to take a dump, either.

He watched the clock. In the oversized mirror on the wall, it teased him with time running in reverse. The stranger stood so still, Robin could hardly tell if it was breathing. Its limbs didn't quaver in the slightest. Robin, however, was starting to get the shakes. He'd worked all day. His body couldn't take much more of this. Fear and exhaustion were blending together.

Finally, he said, "I need a break."

"By all means," it said, and then worried a pointed tooth with its tongue. "If you feel you have time to spare, indulge yourself."

Robin grabbed his cigarettes and backed towards the door. The client made no move to stop him.

"But if you try to run, or call for help, your pretty Aiko will wake up beside your lifeless body. You won't be a pretty sight. After what I would do to you, she would never sleep again."

Robin nodded. He believed every word; was scared shitless that the thing even knew his girlfriend's name.

The tattoo shop was below street level. From the bottom of the stairs, he could just make out the half-moon hanging on its side like a Cheshire grin over the buildings across the street. A few bright stars twinkled merrily in the lightening sky. Oblivious and uncaring to his predicament.

Robin sucked back a cigarette, but it wasn't enough to calm him. He lit another off the dying cherry, flicked the spent butt aside and tried to slow his pounding heart.

His phone sat, heavy, in the side pocket of his army surplus fatigues. He checked his messages; several texts and missed calls. Most of them from Aiko. He didn't respond. He had no reason to believe that the client would let him live—or Aiko for that matter. Robin also didn't want to dwell on how the client had found out about her.

He only smoked half of his second cigarette before dropping it to the cement, grinding it under his boot, and walking back into the shop. Time was running out. Robin hoped all the blood he was injecting under the client's skin would at least give the creepy thing Hep C.

Sweat was running down Robin's brow, chilling him in the cold air. He took a deep breath, staring at his exhausted reflection. *Shit*. Robin re-entered the shop and locked the door. If the thing wanted him dead, he wasn't getting away. Not the way it moved. There was no sense in letting the stranger get anyone else.

"The sun is almost up," the client said.

"I know," Robin answered.

"Time is running out."

"I know."

"For both of you."

"I. Fucking. Know."

He was starting to wish he hadn't drawn the triangles so large, but that was the size of the image on the page. Only the final point to go. He'd saved the maggot-like dick for last, and as he held it loosely in a blue-nitrile-gloved hand, Robin drew the final lines that led halfway down the skinny little thing. This wouldn't the first time he'd had to tattoo a prick. Strangely, he hoped it wouldn't be the last time, either.

Robin ground his teeth as sweat pooled at the tip of his nose and dripped to the floor. He ran the tattoo machine over the thing's body with far greater force than he would have ever used on a human client. A sigh was the stranger's only reaction when Robin finally dropped the machine to the floor—a waste of two hundred dollars he couldn't afford, but he'd never use that one on another person.

"I am not one to renege on a bargain," the client said, smiling. The red lines Robin had etched into his flesh blazed with every heartbeat, almost hypnotizing. "You are safe from me, though I wouldn't go so far to say you are *safe*."

Robin didn't know what that meant and was too scared to care.

"Sunrise," the stranger said, with another deep sigh. It regarded him curiously, taking a measured step forward. Robin stepped back. With that, its pale skin glowed golden. Its hair went from looking razor silver to the red-orange of heated metal. The stranger was so bright, Robin could barely see it. "Home."

And then it was gone, leaving only a heap of discarded clothing lying on top of laceless winter boots and the symbol on Robin's workstation. A pushpin came loose and a photograph Robin had taken of Callan's raven tattoos fell to land on top of the symbol.

Robin nudged the boots with his foot and wondered why the hell he was still at work, and where those clothes had come from.

Robin blinked as the memories finished passing back to him, dropping to all fours in the sand of the volleyball court.

They are creatures of the light and sun, Muninn said. **They are too bright to go unnoticed in the day. Only at night, when the rays of the sun are reflected from the**

moon may they interact with humanity. In the old days they were split, álfar and svartálfar. Light and dark, fair and foul, good and evil. Now, it seems the two have become one.

"Oh, Jesus," Robin moaned. He scrambled on hands and knees. Dimly, Ted heard the artist retching. Not long ago that had been him. He turned his back, to give Robin a measure of privacy. Seeing the elf, feeling the fear he'd imposed in the artist, was an unwelcome reminder of the assault that had welcomed Ted into the Nine Worlds.

Muninn nodded. **Blood. Fear. A prayer to a paper god.**

Ted couldn't go back to what was, and neither could Robin. Not any longer. Ted remembered the satisfaction of getting his hands on the dwarves. Finding Robin a measure of vengeance was the least he could do.

"She's coming," the *álfur* said, wiping thin, blue blood from its face. "She's coming for *you*." The way the *álfur* spoke Ted figured they probably weren't talking about his ex-wife. "You've been warned."

"No, I fucking haven't. Who's coming?"

The álfar were ever as difficult to deal with as the dvergar, Muninn whispered to Ted.

Almost as difficult as you, Huginn added testily.

Ted shook his head, and knelt at the elf's side. "Where's your treehouse, Jack Flash?" In the moment, Ted couldn't think of any elf names to mock it with. At least when he wanted to make fun of dwarves he had seven options.

If he won't talk, perhaps another álfur will, Huginn suggested.

The elf glared and clutched his ribs, wincing at each shallow breath.

"Where's your fucking tree house?" Ted repeated.

"You think highly of yourself if you think you can bull your way through my brothers and sisters," the elf said finally.

"Worked with you, fairy."

"You say what I am, as if it is a curse, or something vile. The word 'man' is used so by us as well. I will not give up my home to you, *Ófriður*. You are a tool of maggots and filth. We know your thoughts on the Nine Realms."

"Nine Realms?" Robin asked.

"Nine worlds in Norse myth," Ted answered. He turned back to the elf. "You. You obviously wanted to say something besides 'hello' and 'fuck you.' Otherwise you wouldn't have got those runes tattooed by the one artist I know in the city." Lightning crackled over the tattoo of Mjölnir and Ted caught a faint whiff of ozone. "What do I have to do to sweeten the pot?"

He looked at the runes Robin had tattooed over the elf's body. Ted recognized two of the symbols without the ravens. *Thurisaz* was the symbol for Thor's hammer—a symbol of protection. The second rune—*naudhiz*—stood for need. And the Norn Skuld's place in the myth cycle. He knew that Norn, the youngest, better as Tilda. She was his girlfriend, for lack of a better term. When he didn't immediately react to the final rune, which looked like an upside down peace symbol, Huginn and Muninn both prompted him.

Alqiz, they said together. Muninn continued alone, **The symbol of Heimdall, defender of the rainbow bridge to Asgard. A very powerful symbol of protection. It also represents the nine times nine choosers of the slain—Odin's valkyries.**

Protection.

Need.

"What are you afraid of?" Ted asked the *álfur*.

He smiled knowingly. "You."

"So you're smarter than you look," Ted answered. "But I don't think that's the warning you came to deliver."

"You've upset a very delicate balance among us."

"Not my idea."

The elf laughed and coughed; shuddering, he forced a smile. "No, I suppose it was not, but you have done so all the same."

It had been the dwarves' plan to give a mortal as much power as they could. They'd chosen Ted, for his temper as much as anything, and sent him out into the world. To stir things up. To pick fights. To bring back the old ways of magic and monsters. His creation had been a reaction to one mad Norn's plan to end all magic on Earth. Ted had conveniently—for the dwarves, if not for him—shown up when he was most needed. Someone who had already been exposed to the creatures and peoples of the Nine. In his case three times.

The golden fucking rule of three.

First there had been the fire giant, Surtur. Second was Tilda. She'd gone against her own blood to take his side. Third was the trickster god Loki, who maybe should've been listed first, as he'd masqueraded as Ted's dog for a time, and then reappeared later to fuck with Ted's life. One of Loki's unexpected appearances had kept Surtur's minions from killing Ted, though Ted had quickly repaid that debt.

"By driving back Surtur, by defying the Norns, many feel you are declaring this land to be yours, that you are setting yourself up as a second All-Father," the elf said.

"Like hell I am."

"Words. Words are meaningless. Your seed is growing even now. A child of the Norn line? One who stands to inherit your power? How could that fail to make us nervous? How could that fail to alter things?"

"That is some crazy shit," Robin said.

"You get used to it."

"What if I don't want to?"

There was the rub. Robin was in for life, which, unless you had the power to defend, usually ended up being a very short span.

Early in the rule of the Norse gods, Odin had built a fence around Midgard—their name for Earth—that had kept the giants, dragons and monsters out. Things slipped through even then, but that remnant of protection was all that kept Ragnarök's survivors, gods and monsters both, from harming the masses of unbelieving humanity.

Unfortunately, as the saying went, *shit happens.*

You could still end up in the wrong place at the wrong time, as Ted had. Or, the right place at the right time, depending on your point of view. Once you've seen magic, there's no going back. You're a part of that world.

The fires started by the explosion of Surtur's coming-out party were still burning now, over a year later. And the giant still crouched at their centre, plotting his escape—and the destruction of the world.

"I'm sorry," Ted said.

"Great, apologize. That'll keep Aiko and me alive." Robin snapped. He shook his head and then dragged his hand over his face, as if trying to wipe the sneer away. When he spoke again, the heat had left his voice. "Since this is your fault, how do you plan on making it up to me?"

How, indeed?

"I didn't know anything when I talked to you. Had I even dreamt… I'd have kept walking past your shop. I shit you not."

Ted looked down at the elf's sword. The hilt looked like it was carved from a human thighbone. The sword's blade shone in the moonlight, reflecting the orb's pale glow, but when Ted touched it the metal was hard and cool to the touch. He handed the sword to Robin, but spoke to the elf.

"Your weapon for your life, Jack."

The elf smiled and hitched himself up into a sitting position. "I can always make another."

Ted thought of the bone hilt, and where—whom—it may have come from. "Then you'd better fucking pray I don't hear about it."

"You like to threaten and bluster," said the *álfur*.

"And I can fucking back it up."

"So could the Aesir, and look what that got them."

Robin was cutting through the air, doing practice lunges with the elf's sword. Ted was surprised. The artist actually looked like he knew what he was doing with the thing. Ted thought about letting the taunt go. He thought about it, and then kicked the elf in the chest, knocking it back to the dirt.

Robin lunged forward with the sword stabbing at the air.

"Under the light of the moon," the elf said, looking pointedly at Ted. "It should cut through anything. Save dragon-scale."

"I'm special that way," Ted said dryly.

"Yes, the *dvergar* did fine work on you. Perhaps we *álfar* should find our own mortal instrument—though I doubt I could make my family agree."

"I don't work for the dwarves."

"You do their work, even if you do not accept their payment. I imagine those misers are even happier to have you in their pocket for free."

"Your protections," he asked again. "Who are they meant to protect you from?"

"Hel," the elf said, whispering the name of Loki's daughter. "She is coming."

"Why are you so afraid of Hel? Aren't elves supposed to be immortal?"

"All the more reason to fear her. What would the ever-living fear more than their end? What else would the goddess of death hate more than that which does not die? She hates us for our life, as she hates those who escape their fates. Her father was supposed to die and join her forever in her hall, but the trickster fooled her, too, as he did everyone else."

The elf was right about that. Loki had found a way out the

ass-end of Ragnarök. Escaping his fate with the same ease he avoided buying his own cigarettes.

"She hates you too, Ófríður. For taking what was once hers."

"I didn't take shit from her."

The Honoured Dead, Muninn reminded.

The elf nodded, as if it had heard Muninn speak. "Yes, you did."

"They weren't hers to hold!" Ted yelled. Gingerly, he rubbed at the golden tattoo of a curving horn on his left shoulder. When he tapped its power, the *einherjar*—the Honoured Dead—were summoned to fight for him. But the *einherjar* weren't the nameless, faceless spirits of long-dead vikings. Somehow the *dvergar* had bound the souls of Ted's family, men who'd fought in the Great War, to the magic of the tattoo. A hell of a way to finally meet one's grandfather.

The elf laughed. "I look forward to you telling *her* that."

"I'll do what I have to."

A fast-moving cloud slid over the moon. The glow faded from the sword in Robin's hand and in the moment when the moon was completely obscured, the elf disappeared. His voice came from the darkness, seemingly from all directions.

"See that you do."

Ted raised his wrist to check his watch. He wasn't wearing it. The watch had broken in a fight with a giant, and had yet to be replaced. But the time must have been after four in the morning. He sighed and wondered if he could sneak back into the house without waking up Tilda.

"Hell is a woman?" Robin asked.

Ted clarified, "H-E-L, one 'l.' She's the Norse goddess of the dead."

Robin digested that thought for a moment before answering. "Right," the artist said nodding. "So… zombies?"

"I reckon so. Ghosts, maybe."

Huginn interrupted their banter. **This is very serious if the queen of Niflheim is moving against you.**

"We'll take things as they come."

"We?" Robin asked.

"Are you in?"

The artist tightened his hands over the bone hilt of his new sword. "Hell, no. I just want my old life back."

Good fucking luck.

2. Baby Let's Play House

Bright morning sun stabbed through the east-facing window of Ted and Tilda's Methville apartment.

"*Ugg*," Ted groaned, rolling over and throwing an arm over his face. *Too early.*

The sun set Tilda's hair alight. When Ted had met her, that hair had been dyed black, now it was iron grey, belying her twenty-three years. Nine simple gold hoops glittered in her left ear, one for each of the worlds; she wore none in her right. For once, she was up before Ted. All she seemed to be wearing was a green and yellow football jersey—his jersey—big enough for her to swim in. No Edmonton Eskimo had ever looked so good.

"Morning, sleepyhead."

There was an edge to her voice. He wondered what he'd done. She was fussing in the kitchen, dishes clinked together. Ted sniffed the air; a hint of carbon, grease, and egg.

"*Buh.*"

"I need to buy you a new watch, Callan," Tilda said loudly to herself, then asked even louder: "You have any idea what time you got home last night?"

He doubted any timepiece would have a long life. Ted yawned and pawed for his cellphone. The fading tan line on his wrist was mostly invisible amidst the tattoos of dragon scales and the

Gjallarhorn that wound around his left arm. He was used to relying on his phone as an alarm clock, but the fucking thing hadn't worked for shit since Loki had given it back to him in Flin Flon. This time the alarm had flip-flopped from a.m. to p.m.

Not that an extra twelve hours of sleep didn't sound like a good idea.

"You sounded like a gods damned thunderstorm when you came in."

"Sorry," Ted mumbled, easing himself upright. "Tried."

He stretched, stiff from another night on the lumpy futon. Funny, he could take a punch from a giant, or shrug off a sword strike, but be near-crippled by a bad night's sleep. Another thing he'd have to call Dwarf Customer Service about. *Not that the number was fucking forthcoming.*

He kept his complaints to himself. Lumpy as the fucking thing was, they only had the futon because of the generosity of Tilda's friend, Melody. Ted had spoken with her over the phone once, when he was newly tattooed. He wondered if ghosts of old loves contributed to his lack of sleep. Til had mentioned the two used to "fool around" but she never did elaborate. Sometimes at night, and especially when Tilda wasn't in the mood—which since they'd moved in together, was most of the time—he wondered whether she and Melody had used this very futon.

Maybe the gift wasn't generosity at all.

The bachelor suite was a shitty little place in a shitty old building, but they hadn't had a lot of options. Vacancy rates in Winnipeg were at an all-time low. Not enough money in renting, Ted figured. Not when apartment blocks were being turned into condos at a record rate. Edmonton had gone through a similar phase some years back.

Features of the suite included a galley kitchen and a washroom with a door. Ted felt like he was back in college again. Cracked plaster was the only art, and his autographed poster of Warren Moon leaned against the wall, hiding a missing length of baseboard. "Tiny" hardly described the cramped apartment, and "shitty" might sue him for defamation for using it to describe the place. Fortunately, neither he nor Tilda had much in the way of possessions. What Ted hadn't given up in his divorce could fit into The Goat—his '68 GTO—and Tilda had spent the last eight years hitchhiking wherever whim or fortune had taken her.

"I made breakfast. You missed it."

He'd been right. There *was* an edge to her voice. He was hungry, but it was a bit of a relief, actually to have missed that meal. She was better at ordering food than cooking it.

"Coffee's on."

Sleep was still creeping around the edges of his intellectual property. He trundled towards the counter and the coffee maker. The dishes hadn't been done. Again. *Goddammit!* They'd been piling up all week. Ted had done them last. It wasn't his turn. He didn't point that out. To do so would mean another fight. Another fight that made him feel like Tilda's father, not her lover. And he certainly didn't need any more reminders that he was almost twice her age.

Swirling his coffee idly, he figured a couple pints of this and a cigarette or three should see him feeling human again. "Thanks, babe."

She smiled. "See if you're thanking me later."

Ted tried to shake the morning fog from his brain. "What's later?"

Tilda's lips pursed tight then snapped open with a soft pop. Ted knew he'd forgotten something important.

"Moving day."

"What?" He shook his head. *Couldn't be. Nothing was packed.* "Today?"

Tilda nodded, once.

Why wasn't anything packed?

"Fuck."

"You forgot." She crossed her arms over her small breasts. The jersey billowed slightly, making the tiny swell of her belly seem larger than it was. She was two months pregnant; almost as far along as they'd known one another.

"I didn't—" Ted sighed. There was no point in lying. "I've been busy."

She wasn't impressed. "I should've bribed the ravens to remind you."

"**But I did remind him,**" Muninn croaked loudly.

Ted winced. The raven tattoo was perched right over his ear, and hadn't the courtesy to whisper. He slapped at his neck. "Thanks a bunch, you fucking Judas."

It *had* reminded him, Ted supposed. Or had at least tried. Then he and Robin had caught sight of the *álfur* and Ted hadn't listened or had forgotten. Not that the distinction would matter to Tilda.

"**The álfar are more worrisome than a clutch of unpacked boxes,**" Huginn offered.

37

Ted didn't thank the raven. Huginn was just trying to one-up its brother bird.

Tilda shot a withering glare at the raven tattoos. Or maybe it was directed at Ted. He chose to pretend it was the birds.

She snapped, "It's a fool's errand. You can't find one of the *álfar*."

Ted couldn't exactly blame her. After two months of searching, he and Robin had found exactly diddly over squat. Until last night.

"And how did your search go?"

That last bit, she'd said lightly, almost sarcastically.

He took a deep breath, about to gloat, but Huginn beat him to the admission.

"**Success!**" the raven exclaimed. Ted groaned. It was too damn early for birds.

"*What?*"

"**Huginn speaks true, Skuld,**" Muninn added.

"Don't call me that. I'm not Skuld. Not anymore." She said the words automatically. Like she'd been rehearsing it in their evenings apart. Like she was trying to bury that single aspect of the Norn she'd been, but was still uncertain who she was. Realization crossed her face as the words of the ravens sank in. "You actually found one of the *álfar*?"

"Freaky little fucker, too," Ted said with a shit-eating grin, pleased to have surprised her—and to have distracted her from her anger. "It went after Robin to give me a message."

"**As for finding, he found us,**" Muninn said, deflating some of Ted's pride.

"You talked to him. What did he say?" Tilda asked, suddenly

intently interested; old argument forgotten, ready to start a fresh one. "Exactly. What did he say, exactly?"

"God, it was like four in the morning when it—he—jumped us. I don't think I can quote fucking verbatim."

Tilda tapped hard against the tattoo of Muninn, who squawked loudly in Ted's ear. Ted flinched even though the jabbing finger didn't hurt.

"Muninn," she demanded. "What did the *álfur* say?"

Ted could feel the ink moving beneath his skin, as if the raven was squirming under the Norn's gaze. "He said: She is coming. She is coming for you."

Tilda wrinkled her nose in confusion. "Who? Who's coming?"

"That is what Theodore asked. And I was getting there," Muninn said, sounding put upon. "When he was questioned further, the álfur admitted he spoke of Hel."

Tilda's coffee mug shook in her hand. Deliberately, she set it down on the counter.

"Hel." Tilda whispered the name. Her voice trembled. It took a lot to scare Tilda. "Hel is coming. For Ted. You're sure that's what the *álfur* said?" She touched a hand to her belly, to their child.

"Yes," Muninn answered.

Tilda's face went ashen. Ted slipped an arm around her waist and pulled Tilda close. "It'll be fine. Andvari made me to kick ass. Hel wants a war, I'll fucking give her one."

"She can't be beaten, Ted. Death always wins. She kept Baldur. She kept the best of the Aesir. She kept—"

"She had some help," Muninn reminded.

"She won't this time," Ted insisted.

"He's her *father*, Ted."

"He" meant Loki. Tilda had been raised to hate the trickster, and still didn't care much for him. She had made something of a peace with him during their adventure in Flin Flon. For his part, Loki only seemed to care about seeing her—or Ted—naked.

"The only way the vikings had to beat her was to die in battle. To live on in Valhalla. But Valhalla's gone. She owns the dead now. All of them. She gets us all, Ted. And she wants you. She wants you dead."

"Yeah." Ted nodded, not impressed. "So does Surtur. So did your amma. And every damn giant in Manitoba. Probably my ex-wife too. A lot of shit wants me dead right now."

"Why didn't you wake me up? Why didn't *you* say something?"

Ted shot back, exasperated, "You're the one who can see the goddamned future! I figured if something important came up, you'd let me in on it."

Tilda shook her head. "You should have known better."

Lately, her precognitive powers had been as unreliable as Ted's phone. Only in Tilda's case the cause was her amma, the Norn Urd, who'd stolen them away, not Loki. After Tilda had been stabbed with a dagger meant for Ted, Urd had given up everything. All the gathered power of the Norns. Future. Past. Present. Urd gave that power to Tilda, hoping it would give her granddaughter the strength to survive. It had. But now, Tilda had to learn to control her visions in the way she had before.

"Hel doesn't piss around. If you thought Loki was dangerous…

If she wants you, she can kill you. She knows how to kill anyone. Everyone. The dead roots of Yggdrasill whisper many secrets. She could finish Surtur if she wanted to."

"Be nice if she'd let me in on that little secret."

"Why does she want you so bad?" Tilda hissed an angry breath. She seemed as mad at herself as she did at Ted. "I didn't see this."

"How do you think the elf found Robin? Shouldn't he have been safe? I didn't use my powers around him."

"You'd been bathed in magic and dragon's blood. You talked about the myths." It was not a question. "Maybe you said or did something you shouldn't have. Something so small you can't remember. Touched by the Nine as you were, the *álfar* could've already had their eye on you. They've warred with the *dvergar* before. You'd never have seen them if they followed you to his shop. Maybe he was caught in that first storm you summoned."

Ted digested the words. What they meant for other innocents.

"Great." Ted dropped his eyes. "It *is* my fault."

"Self-pity doesn't suit you."

Andvari had said the same thing to him before. So had the ravens. Ted was getting a little sick of everyone harmonizing on that note.

"I talked to someone else first. I…" Ted trailed off. Not wanting to bring up Jenny.

She was his best friend's sister, and the person who had picked him up from the Public Safety Building after the police had released him before he started his adventures in mythology. What a clusterfuck his first night in Winnipeg had been.

Dwarves carved Ted up bloody, covering him in tattoos, bouncers had tried to beat him, and yet the cops had arrested *him*. At least the dwarves had also sent a lawyer to spring him. Ted felt bad that he hadn't spoken to Jenny since then. That he'd taken the cheap way out and left her a message when he knew she'd be at work.

I promised to help her. We were going to fix up her house.

And promises are never broken? Muninn asked, speaking in Ted's mind. **You promised your Susanna you would be together forever. What were the words? 'Til death do us part?**

That's a low fucking blow.

In our short time together, I have not noticed you to pay attention to the high road, Muninn said.

Huginn cackled in laughter.

Everybody's a fucking comedian.

Ted shook his head, trying to clear it of the ravens' chatter. He was surprised to find Tilda's hand on his shoulder.

"Jenny's safe," Tilda said. "I don't sense any connection to the Nine within her."

Ted's eyes narrowed. The Norns had manipulated him from the first moment he'd met them. Before the dwarves had even empowered him, the Norns had known of him, and had tried directing his destiny. He couldn't blame Tilda for that. It hadn't been her idea, but her grandmother's. He *did* trust Tilda. But some of Urd was in her now. *How much? And which parts?*

"I went to see her, since you've been so worried. She seems

like a kind woman." For a moment, Tilda's gaze dropped. "And pretty."

"Wasn't that dangerous?" Ted accused.

"She'll be safe, provided *you* leave her be."

Ted tried hard not to take that statement as a threat. "You're sure?"

Tilda nodded.

Ted let out a sigh. "I don't want the Nine Worlds to ruin her life too—"

Tilda's face went hard.

Shit.

"Oh come on," Ted protested. "You know I didn't mean to say it like that!"

"I know exactly what you meant."

"I'm sorry, all right?"

"You pack and load the car. I'm going to the house before the delivery men get there with our new bed. In case you forgot about *that* too."

Nope. Not all right.

"Take a shower before you come over. You stink."

Ted rubbed at his eyes. He didn't need to hear the door slam to know she was gone.

Downtown Winnipeg seemed to have a lot of sketchy streets and their apartment block was on one of them. Not quite as bad as

97th Street back home, but he was glad to be leaving this place behind. Every time he checked, Ted was surprised to find The Goat was still where he'd parked it. The tops of his door locks had been sawed off, but Winnipeg's car thieves didn't use coat hangers anymore.

Ted still couldn't believe how quickly they'd taken possession of the house. Buying a house takes time, even when money like the Norns' is involved, and Tilda had turned out to be surprisingly particular. Between chasing that *álfur* all over hell and creation, Ted remembered looking at eighteen houses in the last month. There may have been more. But this house had been on the market for months. Its old owners were long gone. There were no bidders in all that time. Tilda took one look at the lightning-scarred elm that had canted towards the three-storey house with the peeling brown siding and declared it perfect. To Ted, it looked like he wasn't getting out of doing renovations after all. Money was no issue. The Norns had long memories and had taken full advantage of their visions over the years; Gimli's witches were doing very well for themselves indeed.

But he was still stuck with the handyman's dream home.

Oh, there was a good reason for the fixer-upper. Demolishing old walls and such would give them all kinds of excuses to embed and layer the home with protective runes and enchantments. Just like Grey Ladies, the Norns' teahouse in Gimli, not that Tilda would admit that.

Old elm trees lined the boulevards on either side of the street, vaulting up above the rooftops to create a canopy over the pothole riddled street. Sunlight trickled through bare branches and the leaves that had turned golden, but were too stubborn to fall. He was glad their property had a garage; it would keep the elm sap from gumming up The Goat's paint job.

A three-storey house in this neighbourhood was a long way from their bachelor suite. Ted could tell by the number of cats and damned, dirty hippies that they'd left Methville for the wilds of Winnipeg's granola district. There was even a bongo-playing fucker across the alley. Ted felt like they'd try to ride him out on a rail by Christmas. He smirked. *Good fucking luck to you.*

Smoothing things over with Tilda wasn't going to be easy. He was promised a long rest of his life if an occasional slip of the tongue upset Tilda so much. Maybe she was finally getting hormonal. Though that didn't explain her last two months of irritability. He supposed it was better than referring to the Norns as "myths with tits," a mistake he'd made when he'd first met her family. *Stay classy, Callan.*

He was supposed to do the grunt work. Tilda's pregnancy wasn't too far along, and although she was tough, Ted still worried. She had a casual acceptance that everything would be fine. A vision she'd once had, of them together with their child, was enough to convince her that it would be so. But Urd had also warned that Tilda's viewings of the future were tainted. Spoiled by need and desire. She felt Tilda often saw what she wished to be, not what *would* be. Ted didn't trust Urd. He hadn't even before she'd betrayed him—and Tilda. But her words about the visions had dug in like a fucking tick.

With the strength the dwarves had gifted him, Ted could move boxes all day without tiring. *Hell, I could lift The Goat, and every box stacked within it, if I wanted to.* Not that he would, the neighbours were already giving him the stink-eye—*damn tattoos' fault, no doubt*—and showing off would only damage his car. Or get someone killed.

Even if Tilda had been inclined to schlep boxes, she'd busied herself with another task. When Ted had first walked in, she'd asked him for his pocket knife. The only words she'd said to him since she left the apartment. She was whittling a rune in the oak frame over the front door, singing softly, hips swaying, as if she didn't know he was there. She had a beautiful voice, husky, rather than lilting. A voice for muddy, bluesy rock. No pop princess, her.

Each rune has its own song, Huginn said.

And Skuld knows them all, Muninn added, impressed. **You should listen, instead of watching her ass.**

Something scurried along the baseboard and Ted dropped a garbage bag filled with clothing. "Jesus!" he yelped.

Tilda started. "What?" she asked, turning back to him.

"Mouse," Ted said.

She smiled, stifling a laugh. "*You're* afraid of mice?"

"I'm *not* afraid of them. I think they're filthy and I don't want them in my fucking house."

Tilda seemed nonplussed. "If you've got a stone foundation, you've got mice. One of the reasons so many of our neighbours have cats, I'd imagine. We should get one."

Ted shook his head vehemently. "We are *not* getting a fucking cat. If you want something that hacks shit up and pisses in a box, we can get a fucking hobo. Just because the neighbours have cats doesn't mean *we're* letting one in here. I'll get some poison the next time I'm out."

Tilda chuckled. "For the mice or the neighbours?"

Ted grinned, glad she was laughing again. "Both. I'm gonna have a smoke."

"Outside," she reminded him.

"I know, I know."

Tilda had quit smoking after they'd moved in together. After the baby. It was a bit of a piss off how easily she'd given the habit up. Ted was supposed to be trying too. But he still had a few cigarettes left in that last pack he'd purchased. *When these are done. I won't buy any more.* He almost believed that. How many times had he said those same words? At least Tilda wasn't giving him shit over this. One of the few things they *hadn't* argued about.

"And if you're going to pick a fight with the guy across the alley, try to keep it verbal, eh?"

Ted smiled. "No promises."

Sitting on the back steps of the house, Ted could see their alley neighbour, a skinny beatnik, wasn't in his yard—and neither were the man's bongos. Ted was able to enjoy his cigarette in peace. He mashed the butt into a makeshift tin can ashtray and lit another. Tilda seemed in a better mood, he decided not to spoil it by going inside too soon. Another cigarette seemed the best way to keep her from pecking at him.

A bad turn of phrase, as it turned out.

When are you going to free us again? Huginn and Muninn whined together.

He only let them out late at night and instructed them to be home before morning. Orders that went against their habits and desire. When they had perched on Odin's shoulders, they'd left with the dawn and had flown through the day, like proper ravens. Ted didn't exactly get the lot he'd asked for when he moved to Winnipeg. The uppity birds would have to fucking live with theirs, at least for now.

"I have to be careful," Ted said aloud between drags, not bothering to project a coherent thought at the ravens. Another witness to magic. Another ruined life laid at Ted's feet. "People aren't stupid. If we meet the neighbours and two of my tattoos are suddenly gone, they'll ask questions. Questions I can't answer."

People are stupid, Muninn snapped. **They have always been so.**

You should not be in this place anyway, Huginn added.

Even after two months of their yammering, Ted still found it unsettling when the ravens spoke to him. In a fight that wasn't so bad. Ted kind of liked always having someone watching his back. When he was distracted, he couldn't feel them. Sitting down, smoking, he could actually *feel* the ink moving beneath his skin. And when they spoke to him or when they were agitated they did fucking move, like an itch he couldn't scratch, or million tiny mites hopping in unison. A careful observer would be able to see the beaks of the tattoos opening and closing.

Why did you not take the dvergar's money? Muninn demanded. **It was a gift freely given. Not something they are known for, granted, but you could have been sleeping in a proper bed, not a sitting couch too small for you. You could be anywhere.**

"And you two could be out and flying around?"

Yes, both birds snapped.

"I don't trust Andvari. Or his money." The dwarf owned some big mining and smelting company in northern Manitoba. He'd been the ringleader of the dwarves who'd tattooed Ted. Had even given him a credit card, but Ted hadn't used it. He didn't want to be in their debt. He didn't want to be in *anyone*'s debt. Especially if they were a part of the Nine Worlds. And yet… there was something about that golden card and what it promised. Ted couldn't bring himself to destroy the thing.

I never said to trust him fully. I would never say to trust anyone fully—

"Even you?" Ted said with a smirk.

It was a funny thing to hear a raven sigh. **Sometimes I hate you, Theodore.**

"Don't worry, the feeling's mutual."

Yes. Quite. If you will let me finish this time? Huginn waited for Ted to speak. When he did not, the raven continued. **Do not trust him, but take his money. Take his money and live the life that wealth will allow. If you must live with this Norn, be her equal. Not Loki, begging for handouts.**

Ted hated when the birds made sense. So he changed the subject. "Have you found Loki yet?"

No, Huginn said, suddenly sombre. **I am worried.**

I, as well, Muninn added.

Ted was worried, but about Loki's safety, rather than his activities.

"He's made a lot of enemies." Strangely, he also missed the pain-in-the-ass's company—even if Ted had been the butt of most of Loki's jokes. He was also starting to suspect that Loki had arranged for the dwarves to have him tattooed. And as annoying as the trickster had been, Ted wouldn't have been able to stop Surtur's incursion of Flin Flon without him.

That is not what I meant, Huginn said. **If he is hiding from us, he is clearly up to something. What might it be?**

Ted shrugged. "Dunno." The last he'd seen Loki, the god had been heading north in the shape of a wolf. *Fucking with some-body else's life I imagine. Or just fucking somebody.* He smiled. "Bastard's probably waiting to catch me with my pants down."

A rhythmic *snip* of hedge clippers started up. Across the alley, the neighbour was standing at the edge of his fence, tall and lanky in a way that a stiff breeze could knock over. Ted figured the man was probably stoned. The back of Ted's neck prickled and his skin crawled. He rubbed a hand over his scalp. His hair had grown in with what he felt was a little more grey than red. The dwarves had shaved his body bald as an egg to put the magic tattoos under his skin. At least his balls had finally stopped itching. His neighbour flashed Ted a potent stink-eye and Ted flashed him back with a middle finger before butting out his cigarette and going inside.

With the last boxes inside, and what little they owned unpacked, Ted went to park The Goat in the garage. The new house didn't have much of a backyard. There was a small patch of turned earth that might get enough sun to warrant a vegetable garden someday, and a weed-choked lawn that barely justified purchasing a lawnmower. This property was a far cry from the acreage he and Susanna had once owned. But at least the garage had a basketball hoop.

Ted pressed the garage door opener. It didn't work. He popped the opener off the sun visor and slapped it lightly against his palm; tried again. Nothing. He opened up the battery hatch. Growled. Empty.

Couldn't even leave the fucking batteries.

Ted slid The Goat into neutral and engaged the parking brake. Fumbling to find the right key to manually unlock the garage door, he heaved it open.

"Motherfuckers," he muttered.

The garage was packed, slab to rafters, with every conceivable piece of shit you could imagine. All this shit was *supposed* to be gone. But there it was. A bed's headboard supported a beach pail spilling over with cheap, plastic children's toys. A tangle of vertical blinds, wrapped in ratty old curtains, was on a pile of old and presumably empty paint cans. Old CRT monitors and televisions were stacked like an art installation, crowned with a couple of sewing machines. On the walls were shelves lined with jars of mystery liquid that disappeared into the clutter. Open bags of pink fibreglass insulation had provided a lovely summer home for the mice who were trying to get into the house. The garage smelled of mould, cat piss, and turpentine.

"*Motherfuckers!*"

Ted felt the wind pick up, lifting fallen leaves to swirl in a vortex, scattering them elsewhere. He stood in front of the garage, seething. Trying to get his temper under control before lightning pummelled the garage into a smoking ruin.

"What's going on?" Tilda called from the back porch. "I could hear you yelling from upstairs."

Ted still didn't trust himself to speak. He ground his teeth and exhaled a hissing breath.

"Are you pissed?"

He turned and she read his look quickly enough.

"Good. We're going to Gimli."

Shit. That was no way for Ted to improve his mood.

Tilda's grandmother didn't much care for Ted, and the feeling was mutual. She'd almost got him killed, and without a bit of luck, her plans could've ended the world.

"Urd's not playing ball," Tilda said. She hadn't called the eldest of the Norns "Amma" since she'd woken up in the Flin Flon hospital. "She needs to understand she's not a Norn. Not anymore. Neither is Mom. All they guarded, all they did—it's my responsibility now."

"Ours. We're in this together," Ted said. "What if she won't give that responsibility up?"

"It won't come to that." Tilda sounded certain, but Ted wasn't